The Littlest Tall Fellow

by

Barry Rudner

Illustrated by Thomas Fahsbender

Watercolor by Peggy Trabalka

ISBN 0-925928-00-3

Printed/Published in the U.S.A. by Art-Print &
Publishing Company. Tiny Thought Press is a trademark
and service mark of Art-Print & Publishing Company.
Publisher is located in Louisville, Kentucky 40217
@ 1427 South Jackson St. (502) 637-6916 or
outside Kentucky 1-800-456-3208

Library of Congress Catalog Card Number: 89-84439

Dedicated to my parents

Special thanks to Zack for his patience and support.

There once was a boy
a child so small,
the boy was so tiny
the smallest looked tall.

Knee-high to an ankle,
a weedhopper at heart,
this littlest small fellow,
reached from the start.

2

Chairs and tables,
benches and boxes,
stacks of books
and wood,
a stool or a ladder,
it just didn't matter,
he reached for all
that he could.

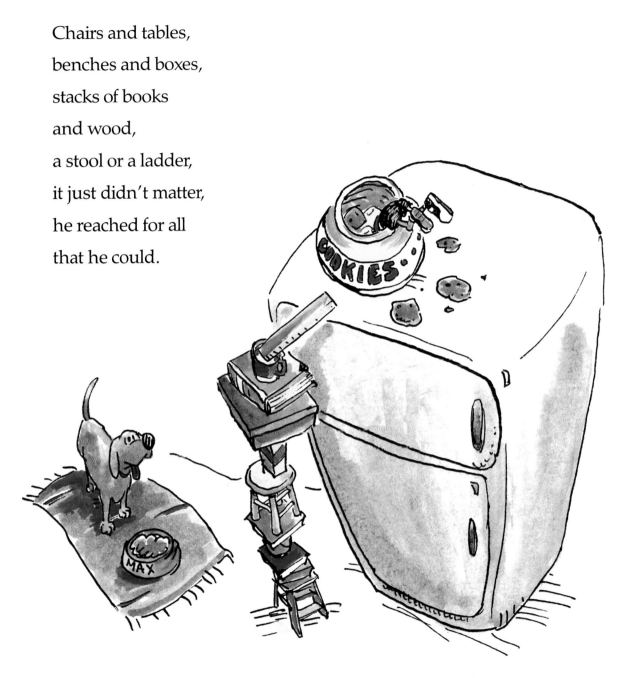

Soon the time came
to go play school,
to learn math and reading
and the golden rule.

There, too, he reached
for all that he could–
the blackboard,
his desk,
his grades,
which were good.

5

Even in sports
he reached for the sky.
But the boy didn't play,
and he couldn't guess why.

"I'm sorry," said the coach,
"You're the size of the ball.
I want you to play.
You're simply too small.
You must stop having
dreams such as these.
People can't always reach
what they please."

Without being noticed,
the boy left the game.
He began to believe
that his size was to blame.

Alone with his thoughts,
he felt the dismay
that maybe his reach
let a dream slip away.

"My size," cried the boy,
"should not matter at all.
Is reaching for dreams
just for the tall?"

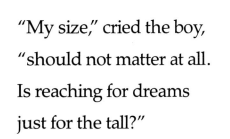

9

He fell to the ground,
a pile of despair.
The boy wished to reach
but he didn't know where.

Then a voice from within
made his eyes open wide.
Instead of high up
his reach turned inside.
The voice told the boy
what he needed to hear
by telling the boy
he had nothing to fear.

"Have you reached," asked the voice,
"with all of your might,
to give up your dreams
without even a fight?
Reaching for dreams
is not about size,
only the courage
of someone who tries."

"To see them blossom
you must help them grow.
Plant your dreams
and never let go."

"So grab each dream
and hold on tight.
And never,
but never,
ever lose sight."

"For dreams are like fruit
to be picked when they're ripe.
They're the sweetest of fruit
and the rarest of type."

"But dreams don't drop
like the fruit from a tree.
You must climb to the top
and pick them, you see.
For those who wait
for their dreams to fall,
rarely, if ever,
reach them at all."

16

The littlest small fellow
listened to the voice
that made him see
he had no choice.

He gathered his courage
and began his long climb,
up to his dreams
one step at a time.

As he reached higher
than ever before
he peered over his shoulder
to the ground once more
to see a small crowd
that began to gather.
He yelled to the crowd,
"Hey! What's the matter?
Why do you people still
stand on the ground?
It's up here!
It's up here!
Where your dreams can be
found!"

But nothing he said
could get them to move.
The boy thought aloud,
"I have something to prove."

He returned to his climb
and at last reached his goal
and grabbed the dream
that he cherished to hold.

With a sigh of relief
he began his climb down
to the now larger crowd
that watched from the ground.
Pleased with himself,
he gleefully laughed,
while the tallest in the crowd
scratched his head and asked,
"How did he do that?
How did he reach?
I'm twice his size
at least by three feet."

The boy smiled at the crowd,
his heart full of pride,
and he silently thanked
the voice from inside.

High in the sky,
the boy held his head,
and with a humble voice
to the crowd he said,

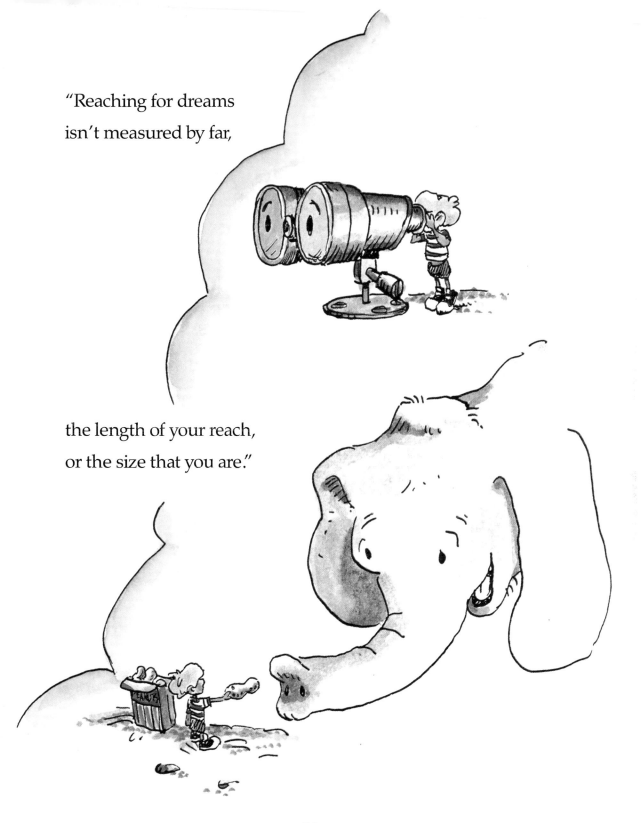

"Reaching for dreams
isn't measured by far,

the length of your reach,
or the size that you are."

"For all that matters
is the strength of your heart.
The size of your heart
will set you apart."

"So if you truly
believe in yourself,
even if you're only
the size of an elf,
and even if you aren't
the tallest at all,
if you reach for your dreams
you'll never be small."

From that day forward

to this very day,

the boy was seen

in a different way.

For the boy who grew taller

without growing one inch,

became THE LITTLEST TALL FELLOW

ever since.

About the Author . . .
Barry Rudner, a Pisces-born twin, was born thirty five
years ago in Detroit where he can still be found to be
growing up.

About the Illustrator . . . . .
Thomas Fahsbender is a sculptor from
New Preston, Connecticut who has never found
a comfortable pair of dress shoes.

About the Publisher . . . . .
Art-Print & Publishing Company (Tiny Thought
Press) would like to hear from
you. Please call us at 1-800-456-3208
and tell us what you think about
"The Littlest Tall Fellow." We are committed
to the enjoyment of children, parents
and grandparents alike.

Other Tiny Thoughts . . . . .

The Bumblebee and The Ram

Nonsense

The Handstand

Will I Still Have To Make
My Bed in the Morning?

Plus others . . . . .